TEAM HERO

THE FROZEN FORTRESS

ADAM BLADE

ORCHARD

MEET TEAM HERO ...

JACK

POWER: Super-strength

LIKES: Ventura City FC

DISLIKES: Bullies

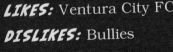

RUBY

POWER: Fire vision

LIKES: Comic books

DISLIKES: Small spaces

DANNY

POWER: Super-hearing, able to generate sonic blasts

LIKES: Pizza

DISLIKES: Thunder

CONTENTS

STORY 1

"WE'VE DETECTED the intruder," said Chancellor Rex through Professor Yokata's Oracle earpiece. "You're cleared to intercept."

"About time," muttered Yokata. She'd been waiting on the rooftop of the Ventura City Museum for most of the day. Chancellor Rex had used his ability to see the future to know that the thief would strike here at some point, the latest in a series of mysterious thefts across the city.

Yokata sprinted across the rooftop of the museum, letting her suspension cord unspool from her belt. At the edge of the skylight she leapt into the air, drew a blaster and fired downwards. The glass exploded inwards as she fell. The marble floor of the main gallery rushed up from below, and just a metre before she slammed into it, the cord went taut and stopped her. Yokata unclipped herself and dropped to the ground, her feet crunching on to glass fragments.

Alarms blared across the room, flashing lights casting everything in a blood-hued glow. It was the museum's medieval exhibit, with suits of armour, weapons and tapestries on display. Straight away Yokata saw she was too late — the case that had once contained a crown was shattered and empty.

But that didn't mean the thief had left. The security door had come down already, sealing off the room. *They're in here, somewhere ...* —

Yokata spun towards the sound of whispered laughter echoing through the gallery. It was hard to tell where it came from.

"Come out!" she said. "You're trapped."

"No, you're trapped," said a female voice.

Yokata's eye caught only a blur of purple movement, an indistinct figure wielding two katana-style swords. Yokata ducked a swipe, then jumped up on to an ancient stone altar. The shape darted across the room, but Yokata pulled forth her second weapon and fired. The stun flare caught the fleeing shape, who tumbled into a heap on the ground.

"If you know me, you know I never miss," said Yokata. "Who are you?"

"Please, don't shoot," said the woman. "I give up."

She lifted one hand in surrender.

"And the other," said Yokata.

The woman's arm whipped out faster than a striking snake and Yokata saw a dagger spinning towards her heart. She dodged, but not fast enough. With a thunk, the dagger embedded itself into the wall, pinning Yokata there through her sleeve. Yokata tore herself free. At the same

time the attacker grabbed the wire still hanging from the skylight.

"Too slow," the thief laughed.

The woman shot upwards with astonishing speed, and vanished.

Yokata holstered her weapon.

"Did you stop the thief?" asked Chancellor Rex in her ear.

Yokata's face burned with shame. "No, sir," she said. "She escaped." She hated letting down the Chancellor.

"This is the fourth theft in as many weeks," he muttered. "What on Earth are we up against?"

"I don't know, sir," said Yokata. She was about to climb back out when she spotted the knife, still jutting from the wall. On its pommel was a strange engraving: an eye wreathed in feathers. "But this time, we have a clue."

CHAPTER 1

THE STORM

THE DECK pitched under Jack's feet as another giant swell rolled beneath the *Lancer*.

They'd been forging a path north for the last day, and were well inside the Arctic Circle. The conditions had been worsening by the hour.

The wave crashed over the ship's bow

and threw spray at the front shield of the bridge. The *Lancer* was one of Team Hero's most high-tech exploration vessels, and built to withstand the toughest of conditions, but that didn't mean it was always a comfortable ride.

We're on a mission though. No turning back now.

The key had been the dagger. Though Professor Yokata had failed to stop the theft at Ventura City Museum, the culprit had slipped up and left the knife behind. Jack remembered the shape of the engraving well — an eye, open wide, with feathers for lashes. It had meant nothing to him, but Chancellor Rex had turned quite pale when he saw it. "The Sisterhood," he'd whispered. "I thought they'd all gone."

"Looks like they're back," the Professor had said. She'd then explained in the briefing that the Sisterhood were an ancient organisation based deep in the Arctic Circle. Once they'd been allies with Team Hero against the underworld forces of Noxx, but it was believed they'd disbanded after the conflict ended.

A door swished open, and in strode Captain Harrah, followed by a couple more crew members in uniform.

"Nothing like a bit of weather to get the heart pumping, eh?"

"It's Danny's stomach that's about to start pumping," said Ruby. She was sitting beside the navigation console.

"Not all over my bridge, I hope!" said the Captain.

"Maybe we should turn back to calmer waters," groaned Danny.

"Nonsense," said Harrah. "Stay on course."

"Sir," said Ruby. "Hull tolerance is near maximum. We take a big hit now, and it could cripple us."

Captain Harrah reddened. "Are you an Admiral, girl?"

"Er... no sir,' said Ruby.

"Then you don't outrank me?"

"No, sir."

"Then keep your landlubber opinions to yourself!" screeched Harrah.

The navigator checked her monitors. "Sir, we've got ice forming over some of the communications array. At this rate, we'll lose contact with Team Hero HQ in a matter of minutes."

A console began to flash. "We've just lost radar and sonar," said the navigator. "We're sailing blind."

The ship lurched.

"Switch to manual controls!" said Harrah. The woman tapped her screen, and from the floor a large wheel rose up. Harrah gripped the handles, like an old-fashioned seafarer. "Any good news for me?"

A horrible retching sound came from behind the monitors, and Danny looked up, wiping his mouth.

"I managed to get it in the bin this time!"

Captain Harrah rolled his eyes. "Remind me to have a word with Chancellor Rex about the quality of the Team Hero sea training. I've never met such a bunch of pathetic—"

"Sir!" said Danny, his long ears suddenly pricking up. "I hear something. Something big." He pointed out to starboard.

"Magnify!" said Harrah.

The viewing screen zoomed into the

distance, and Jack saw a mountain jutting from the sea. Only it wasn't a mountain. It was moving towards them. *Tsunami!*

"Scanning ..." said the navigator. "Data indicates the wave is one hundred and four metres high, containing chunks of ice weighing up to thirty tonnes each." She turned to Harrah. "The hull can't take that sort of impact, sir."

Even Captain Harrah looked worried now. "Comms, open shipwide channels."

The man at the comms console obeyed.

"This is your captain speaking," roared Harrah. "All crew, batten the hatches. It's going to be a rough ride."

He spun the wheel, and the nose of the *Lancer* lurched around, almost throwing Jack from his seat. Something banged deep below, followed by a lurch.

"Port stabilisers have gone!" yelled the helmsman. The wheel began to turn the other way, and Captain Harrah struggled to hold it. Then the ship hit another breaker and the wheel spun from his hands, hurling him across the room.

"Captain!" cried Jack.

Harrah looked dazed. "Shiver me timbers!" he said. "We need to meet the wave head on or it's Davy Jones's locker for all of us!"

Jack undid his seatbelt and ran to

the spinning wheel as the ship was tossed around in bone-juddering jerks. Concentrating all his strength, he gripped the handles, and his hands glowed gold as they took the strain.

He could see the wave clearly, looming larger by the second. They were almost side on — the worst possible place to be. At impact, the weight of water would capsize and swamp them in an instant.

Gritting his teeth he forced the wheel in the opposite direction. Slowly — too slowly — the *Lancer* came around.

"One hundred metres till impact!" shouted the navigator. "Come on, Jack!"

"You can do it!" said Danny.

Jack's shoulders burned as he pulled at the wheel, and he felt they'd either burst from the sockets or the wheel itself would break beneath his grip. Little by little he turned it, and the bow of the ship turned towards the wave.

"Fifty metres!" shouted Ruby, looking over the navigator's shoulder.

They were still only halfway turned to meet the wave. Jack closed his eyes and heaved. He felt the nose of the vessel begin to lift as the wave front slid beneath them.

He braced his legs and with a final roar gave all his strength to the effort. The bow rose. He opened one eye and

saw they were shooting up the wave,
steeper and steeper until they were
almost vertical and it seemed certain
the wave would tip the entire ship over
backwards. Chunks of ice slammed
into the ship's hull, and a crack split
the shield.

CHAPTER 2

SHIPWRECKED

THE BOW of the ship burst into
open air, and for a moment Jack felt
completely weightless, his stomach
climbing into his throat.

And then they were falling down the
far side of the wave, picking up speed.

"Brace yourselves!" he cried.

They plunged down into the sea, and

Jack gripped the wheel as the impact shook the bridge so hard he thought it might break apart completely. Sea water swamped the entire front of the ship, before natural buoyancy brought her level again. Icy water was spraying through the crack in the front shield.

But the seas were calmer here on the other side of the wave.

"Damage report," said Captain Harrah, picking himself up from the floor.

"Comms are down," said Ruby. "Navigation's down. Stabilisers have gone; engines one through three are non-functioning."

"We've got leaks through hull breaches on decks three and five," said Danny.

"Rudder's sheered off completely," added Jack, analysing the diagnostic panel. He turned to Harrah. "We're basically a floating raft."

"And at the mercy of the waves," said Captain Harrah grimly.

For the next few minutes they simply stood their ground as the sea tossed the *Lancer* this way and that. Messages came through from the rest of the vessel, detailing injuries to the crew and damage to the ship. The internal heaters had obviously been damaged, because the temperature on the bridge plummeted until Jack could see his own breath in clouds.

"We need to fix the communications array," said Harrah, hugging himself for warmth. "If we can get a message to the nearest Team Hero outpost, they'll be able to send help."

"Uh-oh," said Ruby, squinting through the front shield. "Look!"

For a moment, Jack's heart froze. *Another giant wave!*

But then he realised this one wasn't moving. A giant island of rock rose from the sea, tipped with steep snow-clad

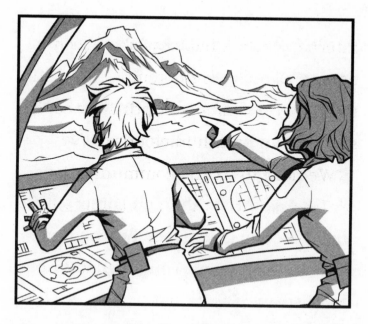

mountain peaks. "Land ahoy, Captain!"

A moment later the deck shook
violently with a horrible screeching
sound and the ship stopped dead as it
ran aground.

"Guess we won't need the anchor,"
said Danny.

"Where are we?" asked Jack looking at the island ahead.

Ruby checked the charts. "With the satellite link down, there's no way to know," she said.

"OK," said Harrah. "You three, suit up. Take the emergency beacon and get to a high point. You should be able to raise an SOS."

"What about you, sir?" said Danny.

"A captain doesn't leave his bridge," said Harrah. "I'll stay and direct the crew in repairs. You'll have to do this on your own."

Jack, Ruby and Danny went to the storeroom and donned the Team

Hero thermal gear that could protect wearers in temperatures as low as minus thirty degrees. That was good, because Jack could hear an Arctic wind howling outside.

"Look on the bright side," said Danny. "At least we'll be on solid ground."

The emergency beacon was in a small rucksack, which Jack put on his shoulders.

Ruby slung her mirrored shield over her back.

"Will we need weapons?" asked Danny.

"Better safe than sorry," said Jack.

He strapped Blaze to his waist too. Danny shouldered his energy bow.

They lowered the ramp of the vessel on to rocky shallows. Their waterproof boots kept their feet dry as they clambered on to the island, which looked like a barren waste of rock and ice. There was no vegetation at all among the patchy snow.

The three friends trekked up a rocky gully filled with a frozen streams, then crossed a slope of loose scree. The wind whistled around them, occasionally buffeting hard enough to make them stumble. Blizzards of snow whipped past, but inside his suit, Jack was sweating.

"How much further?" said Danny.

Jack glanced up at the mountain peak ahead. Above the lower reaches, the slope steepened to an almost vertical cliff-face. "Hawk, how high do we need to go?"

In his ear, his Oracle replied, ***"To ensure the beacon's signal reaches the nearest Team Hero outpost, you will have to achieve an elevation of 1,129 metres. The top, basically."***

"Not far," Jack lied to Danny.

"Remember the last time we were on an island, guys?" said Ruby. "We met Dr Maranya."

Jack shuddered at the memory. The Team Hero scientist had gone mad and turned herself into a spider-human hybrid.

"Thanks for reminding me," said Danny. "I hate spiders."

"At least that was a *tropical* island," said Ruby, wiping snow from her visor.

There was a vertical slash in the rockface ahead, and they stepped inside to take shelter. At once, the wind dropped. The passage between the two sides was steep, but the ground had formed into deep steps and they climbed in single file.

Halfway up, Jack saw strange lines

carved into the ice walls.

Almost like slash marks.

"You think these are natural weathering?" he said.

"This place can't be inhabited, surely," said Danny from behind.

They reached the top of the scar, and all stopped. The steps continued, some covered in ice and snow, up the slope ahead. There could be no doubt someone had made them.

"Maybe *Lancer* stayed on course after all," Jack said. "This could be the island of the Sisterhood."

"We'd better be on our toes, then," said Ruby, at his side.

They trudged side by side through thicker powdery snow up the slope until they reached a sheer cliff-face.

"Hawk, are we high enough to launch the emergency beacon transmitter?" asked Jack.

"Negative," said his Oracle.

Jack look up the rockface with a sinking feeling. But then his eyes snagged on a small crevice, just a metre or so up. There was another just above. "Are those ... handholds?"

"I think so," said Ruby.

"I'd prefer an elevator," said Danny.

With Ruby in the lead and Danny second, they began to climb, hand over hand. Some of the holds were slippery with ice, and the gusting wind threatened to hurl them to their deaths. Jack made sure his grip was secure before moving off to the next anchor points. After fifteen metres or so, he looked down, and wished he hadn't.

At a sheer section, with an overhang, the handholds traversed the slope, so they were climbing sideways rather than upwards. The distance between the crevices seemed to increase and Jack had to reach further for each, straining his joints. *Whoever made these must be either very tall or very flexible!*

Ruby had to jump to snatch the next grip above, and for a moment she dangled from two hands before her feet found purchase. "Careful, Danny," she said.

Their friend looked worried as he reached the same spot. Jack saw him tense, then push off. One hand caught a hold, the other fell a fraction short. With a cry, Danny fell.

Jack reached out by instinct, grabbing his friend's sleeve. His fingers on the rock glowed gold, but it didn't matter as they slid off the ice.

He was falling too.

CHAPTER 3

THE SECRET DOOR

JACK HIT the ground before he
expected, the air punched from his
lungs. Beside him, Danny groaned.
Jack realised they'd been lucky enough
to hit a narrow ledge. When he peered
over the side, the drop was dizzying.

"Jack? Danny?" Ruby called down.

"We're all right," Jack called back.

He sat up, brushing the snow from his suit and wondered how they could climb back up.

But Danny was staring past him. "Jack, look!"

There was an archway, carved right into the rockface, and sealed with a rough stone door.

"Ruby!" called Jack. "Get down here!"

She picked her way towards them carefully, then dropped to their side.

"Weird place for a door," said Danny.

"I guess they don't like visitors," said Ruby. "Do we knock?"

Jack placed his hands on the stone, and directed his strength into his fingers. Bracing himself, he was surprised when the door slid sideways easily. Warm air bathed his face. They stepped into a wooden porchway. As soon as they'd crossed the threshold the stone door thunked closed behind them. It wasn't quite pitch black, and with their Oracles' night-vision, everything had a green tinge. Danny tried the stone door again, but it didn't move.

"It's locked," he said.

They faced an inner set of double doors made of rough-hewn timbers. Across the centre was carved a symbol Jack knew well — an eye surrounded by feathers.

"This is definitely the thief's base," Ruby whispered.

Danny pushed open the interior doors, ears twitching. On the other side was a vast open courtyard, lit not with torches, but with what seemed to be glowing red stones like solidified lava, sitting in nooks on the walls. Scaffolding of wood and elevated walkways ran around the perimeter, leading into various tunnels and archways cut directly into the rock. In the centre of the courtyard was what looked like a stone well, and steam rose from within.

"I think this place must be geothermally powered," said Ruby.

They had walked along one of the wooden bridges a few steps when Danny put his finger to his lips. They all crouched instinctively as a single tall woman in baggy violet robes exited one of the tunnels, carrying a basket in front of her. Luckily she wasn't coming in their direction, and disappeared through another door.

One of the Sisterhood? Jack wondered.

As they neared a tunnel entrance, Danny paused again. "Listen! Can you hear that?"

Jack closed his eyes and strained his ears. There was a sound, dim and distant. It sounded like chanting voices, but he couldn't make out any of the words. It seemed to be coming from the tunnel mouth in reverberating echoes. He drew Blaze from his sheath, and led the way into the corridor. More of the glowing stones illuminated the route, bathing everything in a blood-red shade. Tapestries hung on the walls, showing ranks of identical spindly figures in what looked like sacred processions, or worshipping at the foot of a mountain. The chanting grew louder, until, at the end of the corridor, they came to a balcony overlooking a large chamber.

There were thirty or forty women below, taking part in synchronised martial arts manoeuvres — kicks and punches and chops. They moved fluidly, their purple robes swirling about them. It looked almost like a dance, but the power of their strikes was clear. With each blow they shouted or grunted.

What kind of place is this?

One thing was for certain: he didn't fancy their chances against the well-drilled army below.

Jack and his friends crept along the balcony, and into an adjoining corridor. It led to another chamber, this time on their level. There were doors in the other three walls as well. In the centre there was a small plinth, and around the edges were stationed a dozen or so wooden dummies. It looked like they were supposed to represent people, with simple trunks

for bodies and protruding pieces of
timber to represent arms and legs.
The strangest thing was the grooves
crisscrossing the floor. Jack, Ruby
and Danny made their way to the

plinth, looking for clues. On the top, carved into the stone, was the imprint of a hand. Danny spread his fingers and laid his hand over the indentation.

"Maybe don't touch," said Ruby. "We don't want to set off an alarm."

"I don't see any wires," said Danny, laying his hand over the indentation. "I'm sure it'll be absolutely..." The doors on the walls all slid closed at once. "...fine?" said Ruby, with a sigh.

From the corner of his eye, Jack saw movement. One of the wooden dummies turned on the spot, then lurched from the side of the room towards them. Its arms swung like clubs. One by one, the others came to life as well.

"Great!" said Jack. "This couldn't get any worse!"

With a grinding sound, metal walls rose up through the grooves in the floor. Jack jumped back as one sealed him off from his friends. He found himself looking along a passageway formed by the walls. *It's a maze ...*

"You were saying?" said Ruby, from the other side of a wall.

Jack heard the combat dummies rolling closer. "Weapons ready!" he shouted. "They're coming!"

CHAPTER 4

THE SISTERHOOD

JACK HEARD a noise behind him, and something clubbed him on the back, sending him flying into a barrier. As he turned and lifted his sword, he saw a wooden dummy attacking him. The dummy hit his arm, knocking his sword to the ground. The dummy advanced, arms punching, but Jack managed to grab them both in his scaly fists. He wrestled with the powerful contraption, then with a cry pulled the arms from their sockets. Sparks showered over him as the dummy spun around, malfunctioning.

Jack picked up his sword, ran around the bend and found Ruby in another passage.

"Where's Danny?"

"Over here!" called his voice. They ran towards the end of their passage, but another dummy was waiting, chopping up and down with its arms. Ruby rammed her shield into it, smashing it to pieces. They took a couple of twisting paths, Jack in the lead. As he rounded the corner, Ruby yanked him back just as one of Danny's energy arrows pierced the wall right where his head would have been.

"Thanks!" Jack said to Ruby. He raised his hands. "Don't shoot, Danny — it's us."

"Sorry!" called Danny. "Thought you were one of them!"

"We need to get out of the maze," said Ruby.

With a clunking noise, a fighting dummy lumbered towards them. Jack cut off one of its arms, then grabbed its featureless head. With a twist, he

snapped it around one hundred and
eighty degrees, then shoved it away,
sending it crashing into another of its
kind. The dummies then proceeded to
attack each other.

Huh, they are pretty dumb.

Jack, Danny and Ruby left them
to it, and went in the other direction.
Through trial and error, and taking
out the dummies on the way, they
finally passed through a door and
stumbled back out into the room.
As soon as they did, the maze walls
dropped behind them, revealing the
strewn wooden carcasses, some
limbless, some burnt, and some

smashed into several pieces.

"Well, that was fun," said Danny.

"I'm glad you enjoyed yourselves," said a voice.

They all spun around to see, on the balcony above, a number of purple-clad warrior women. Ruby stepped in front and raised her shield.

"Don't bother," said the leader. She had a mane of wild red hair, skin the colour of mahogany, and eyes that appeared to be all pupil — black within black. "We could have killed you the moment you sneaked in, had we wished."

"Yeah, well, we dealt with your puppet army easily enough," said Ruby.

"The maze is designed for our children to practise hand-to-hand combat," said the woman, with a barely concealed sneer. She clicked her fingers and Jack heard the flap of wings overhead. A falcon with ice-blue feathers landed on the woman's shoulder.

"Who are you?" asked Ruby.

The woman glared. "Normally it would be the uninvited guests who answered questions. I am Mercia, and these are my sisters. Now tell me, why shouldn't we kill you?"

Danny pulled back an arrow on his bowstring. "I'd like to see you try."

Mercia smiled in a not altogether

friendly way. "You have a great deal
of fear in you." She lifted her face.
Two beams of black energy shot from
her eyes, and poured into the corner
of the room. Something took shape

in the shadows: a bulbous body, with several huge hairy legs. *A spider!* They were one of Danny's worst fears, and this one was as big as a car.

Danny wailed as the giant arachnid scurried up the wall and jumped right on top of him. "Get it off me!"

"No!" cried Jack, slashing at the huge creature with his sword, but the blade passed right through the spider, meeting no resistance. He swiped again, with the same effect.

A projection!

"It's not real, Danny," said Ruby. "It's just a trick."

"I can feel it!" he cried.

"My, my," said one of the other women. "You are making a fuss."

Jack looked at the person who'd spoken. He recognised the voice but couldn't see her face. As she stepped from the shadows, he drew a sharp breath at the slim, dark-skinned form of a woman in her early twenties.

"Serenade!" he cried.

She scowled at him. Serenade — or the Silent Shadow as she was also known — was a mercenary for hire, and had been an ally of their enemy, the Agent. One hand rested on the hilt of her katana sword.

But what's she doing here?

CHAPTER 5

FIGHTING SHADOWS

DANNY WAS still cowering on the ground, but Mercia waved a hand and the giant spider collapsed into black smoke. Danny peered out between his fingers, the whites of his eyes open wide.

"Has it gone?"

"That was terrible thing to do!" Ruby said to Mercia.

Serenade laughed. "I thought you were Team Hero, not Team Coward."

Ruby's eyes glowed as she advanced. "Let's see who's a coward, shall we?"

Serenade drew her nano-sharpened blade from its sheath but Mercia stepped between them.

"Not yet, my protégé," she said. "We need answers." Turning to Jack, she asked, "How did you find this place?"

"Their doddery old headmaster can see the future," said Serenade. "No doubt that's how they knew I was going to attack the Museum. He must have led them here as well."

"Don't speak about Chancellor Rex

like that," said Danny. "He's a good man and a fine leader."

"I've heard of this power before, but never truly believed it," said Mercia, arching an eyebrow. "Think what I could achieve with such an ability!"

"Actually," said Ruby. "It wasn't Chancellor Rex. We were following a clue we found at the museum — a dagger with an eye carved into it. The symbol led us here. I suppose you're the so-called Sisterhood?"

Mercia wheeled to face Serenade. "You must have dropped your weapon, you careless fool!"

Serenade flinched. "I ..."

"You're an embarrassment to the Sisterhood," said Mercia. "First you fail the Agent, then you give away the location of our base!"

"I was at the museum on your orders," replied Serenade. "You said it would be a simple job, but Team Hero

were waiting for me."

"And you failed to adapt to the situation," said Mercia. "Enough of your excuses. You must redeem yourself or be sent into exile."

"Sister," said one of the other women. "Perhaps you are being too harsh. Serenade is a good—"

"Silence!' said Mercia. "I have passed my judgment. Serenade has one last chance to remain with us."

"Anything," said Serenade, bowing.

Mercia smiled cruelly, as her eyes settled on Jack. "You must fight our intruder in single combat," she said. "Form a circle, sisters."

"Wait!" said Ruby, but before she could do anything, a metal helmet from one of the wooden dummies was thrust over her head and clamped at the neck. *To neutralise her eye-beams*, thought Jack. Danny was seized too, his arms wrenched behind his back. Jack watched helplessly as his friends were dragged to the doorway. The rest of the women, meanwhile, fanned out into a circle, surrounding him and Serenade.

"Whoever is knocked from the circle first loses," said Mercia. She raised a hand. "Ready ... fight!"

Jack and Serenade drew their swords and the gleaming blades reflected the torchlight. Jack felt a tingle of fear. He'd seen Serenade fight before — he knew her powers of speed and precision. Using her special ability, she shot towards him faster than his eyes could follow and he lifted Blaze instinctively to parry. The clash of metal showered sparks over the timbers of the floor.

"Lucky block," said Serenade.

Jack thrust towards her, but she was gone in a blur, reappearing at his side. She swiped with an upwards cut, and pain shot through his shoulder. Just a nick, but she could easily have severed his arm if she'd wished.

Is she holding back? Why?

As he tried to block her next blow, she caught his wrist. With a cry of pain, he dropped Blaze to the floor. Serenade leaped over the top of him in a blur, and before he could turn fully, she side-kicked him under the ribs and hurled him through the air. He slid across the floor, winded.

"Finish him," said Mercia.

Serenade advanced more slowly, her gaze steely. Jack's sword was out of reach and as she stabbed, he raised his arm and caught her blade in his fist. His power flowed into the scales of his hands, gripping the katana hard. Serenade leaned into him with all her weight, but Jack was stronger. "I don't want to hurt you," he said through gritted teeth.

"You couldn't if you tried," she snarled.

She continued to press, so with his free hand he ducked and turned, letting her fly over his hip in a judo throw. The circle parted as Serenade crashed into the crowd, landing on her back with a hard thump. Her katana clattered to the ground beside her.

"Jack wins!" shouted Danny.

Serenade scrambled to her feet. "He used his powers!"

"So what?" said Ruby. "You used yours!"

Serenade snatched up her sword, but Mercia stood in the way and shook her head. The black rays shot from her eyes again as a glass tube appeared around Serenade's body. She looked afraid.

"You couldn't even defeat a child!" said Mercia.

From the bottom of the cylinder, water began to bubble up around Serenade's ankles, though Jack couldn't work out where it was coming from.

First the giant spider and now water. What kind of special ability is this?

Serenade screamed in terror as the water rose up her chest.

"Stop that!" cried Ruby. The Sisters

had removed the helmet they'd put over her head, but they still held her back. "It's not right!"

"Serenade has failed us for the last time," said Mercia, her gaze pitiless.

The water level reached Serenade's chin, and she tipped her head back to breathe. Jack couldn't watch for another moment, and raised his fist to smash the cylinder apart. Suddenly Mercia snapped her fingers and the cylinder vanished.

Serenade fell to her knees, completely dry, but sobbing.

"Take the prisoners to the cold cells," snapped Mercia. She pointed at Serenade. "All of them."

STORY 2

CHANCELLOR REX was seated in the control room at the Team Hero HQ when Yokata looked across from her console.

"Incoming message, sir," she said. "The source is close to the *Lancer*'s last known position."

Rex sat forward in his chair. They'd lost touch with the Team Hero flagship around five hours before.

"Put it through," said Rex.

On the screen, the face of a woman appeared. She was standing in front of a rocky wall, and flickering light cast shadows over her fierce, angular features. But it was her purple robes that gave her away — she was one of the Sisterhood.

"Greetings, Chancellor," she said. "My name is Mercia. I will keep this brief. Three of your students have washed up on our shores. They are ... badly injured. I fear at least one of them will die without urgent medical care."

"Tell us your position," said Rex. "We'll send help at once!"

The woman called Mercia shook her head. "The Sisterhood are mistrustful of strangers, Chancellor. We will allow a single visitor."

"Of course," said the Chancellor.

"Then I will come myself."

"Very well," said Mercia. "I've sent our coordinates."

The transmission ended suddenly.

"I've received the coordinates," said Yokata, "but … do you think this is safe? It might be a trap."

"What choice do we have?" said Rex. "If the students are in danger …"

He stood up, lifted his hands, and summoned forth a vision of the future. In the smoky tendrils that extended from his open palms, an image appeared. It was hard to make out at first, but as he focused his power, he realised it was a boy, floating upright in the water, his limbs limp and lifeless. His Team Hero gear was torn.

It can't be ... thought Rex.

But the scaled hands confirmed it. *Jack.*

He let the vision fade and saw Yokata was equally distraught. "That settles it," he said. "I have to go ... now!"

CHAPTER 1

THE COLD CELLS

JACK HUGGED himself, shivering as a freezing wind whipped past through the ice ravine. The cold cells weren't cells at all, but they didn't need walls. He, and each of his friends, plus Serenade, were perched on four separate metal platforms a hundred metres up, and supported by narrow poles in the centre, like lofty spinning plates. There was no way down. The Sisterhood had removed their thermal gear, leaving them in just their regular bodysuits. Danny's lips were blue. Jack jumped up and down, trying to get the blood flowing.

Only Serenade seemed untroubled. On her platform, she sat cross-legged with her eyes closed.

"The tips of my ears are going to get frostbite soon," grumbled Danny.

"I've got an idea," said Ruby, teeth chattering. She focused on the metal plate beneath Danny and blasted it with fire-beams.

Danny stretched out his hands. "It's working, a bit."

Ruby warmed Jack's next, then her own. A few waves of warmth rose around Jack, before the howling wind snatched it away.

"Save your energy," said Serenade, opening one eye. "It'll get much colder when night falls."

"Maybe you could, y'know, tell us how to get out of here," said Ruby.

"There is no way out," said Serenade. "That's the point of the cold cells. The platforms can only be lowered from the controls at the base of the poles."

"What about the walls?" said Jack, pointing to the sides of the ravine.

"Even if you could reach them, they're sheer ice," said Serenade. "You couldn't get any grip, even with your weird hands."

Charming, thought Jack.

"So we just sit up here until we turn into human ice cubes?" said Danny.

"That's about it," said Serenade. "Despite her name, Mercia isn't very merciful."

"So why are you in her gang?" snapped Ruby.

Serenade sighed. "She wasn't the leader when I joined," she said. "We lived by a gentler code then. But when Mercia took over, it changed. She's more interested in power and riches."

"Like a certain museum thief we know," muttered Danny.

Serenade turned away, as if ashamed. "You're right, in a way. I let myself be led by Mercia, because the Sisterhood are the only family I know. I'd be dead without them."

"What's with her power?" asked Danny. "That spider thing was like something out of my nightmares."

"Exactly," said Serenade. "Mercia is able to create illusions that tap into our deepest fears."

"But they're just hallucinations?" said Ruby. "Not that scary."

"The person affected feels it like it's real," said Serenade.

"And your fear is drowning?" asked Jack gently.

Serenade nodded. "When I was a little girl, my family were wiped out in a flood. The Sisterhood rescued me and took me in."

Serenade's family died in a flood, so that's why Mercia used her power to make it seem like she was drowning.

Jack was horrified.

He rubbed his chest to try to stay warm, but he knew it wouldn't be long before hypothermia set in. He knew from their lessons what happened then. The body and mind would slowly shut down. They might see hallucinations too, which would cloud their judgement. It wasn't beyond the realms of possibility that they'd jump off the platforms to their deaths, believing there to be a pool of warm water below.

Ruby blasted the platforms again, driving the temperature up for a few seconds. Jack laid his numb hands on the metal. Suddenly he had an idea.

"I think there might be a way down," he said to the others. "If we can get to the ice wall—"

"I told you, it's too slippery," said Serenade.

"What if we could create some handholds?" said Jack.

Ruby appeared to understand. "Great plan!" she said.

Focusing on the walls, she shot a short blast of flames, melting a section of the wall and leaving a steaming indentation.

"One handhold," she said.

Repeating the action, she created another just below. Then another. Serenade watched, a small smile creeping over her lips.

Jack stepped to the edge of his platform. It was at least six metres to the wall of the ice canyon.

"You can't make it," warned Danny.

Jack swallowed. Even with a run-up, he realised Danny was right. His legs weren't powerful enough to jump the distance.

But there might be another way …

"Serenade, if you can get to my platform, I could throw you."

The woman frowned. "How do I know you won't just hurl me to my death?"

"Because I'm not a murderer," said

Jack. "Plus, we need you to operate the controls at the bottom to lower the platforms."

Serenade still looked suspicious.

"Come on!" urged Danny.

"All right," said Serenade. She sped towards the edge of her platform and leapt off. She landed by Jack, and he grabbed her to help keep her steady.

"Ready?" he said, gripping her cold hands in his.

"Do it!" she said.

He spun round then let go, tossing her off the platform. She screamed as she flew through the air, then hit the wall. For a moment, she slipped, then

her hands locked into the holds.

"Never in doubt," said Danny, though his face was pale with fear.

Serenade began to pick her way carefully down.

"She trusted you," said Ruby, "but can we trust her?"

"She's our only chance," Jack said. Serenade's shape became smaller and smaller as she descended, then the blizzard swallowed her.

Several minutes passed. Jack couldn't feel his feet or his hands now. Danny was visibly trembling with cold, and even the fire in Ruby's eyes was beginning to fade.

We've made a terrible mistake, thought Jack. *Serenade's abandoned us, and we're going to die up here.*

The worst thing of all was that they'd failed the mission. There was no way even to get word back to Chancellor Rex at the Academy about the threat Mercia posed.

Under his feet, the platform shook and juddered, then slowly began to descend. Looking across, he saw those of the others doing the same, and his heart leapt.

"She did it!" said Ruby.

The platforms reached the ground level, where the former member of the Sisterhood waited for them.

"Now," she said grimly, "are you ready for the hard part?"

CHAPTER 2

MERCIA'S PLAN

SERENADE LED them out of the wind, and into a chamber filled with rotten food.

"Gross!" said Ruby, holding her nose.

"This is where our waste is sent to decompose," said Serenade. "We harvest the bio-matter to power our transport and comms systems, in addition to geothermal energy from under the island."

Serenade pointed to an opening in the wall above the pile of kitchen scraps. "Channels run throughout the habitation. It's the only way we can get around without being detected."

"So we're climbing through the trash chute?" asked Ruby.

Serenade nodded. "We can get to the vehicle bay and escape from there."

Jack grabbed the edges of the chute and pulled himself inside. The stench was almost overpowering, making his eyes water. He reached down and helped the others up as well.

"I'm so glad my power is super hearing and not super smelling," said Danny.

The tunnels were carved into bare rock. There were dozens of branches leading off at different angles, like a giant termite mound, and Serenade led the way. Sometimes it was hard to tell if they were heading up or down.

"Are you sure you know where you're going?" asked Danny.

Serenade stopped to peer through a grate. "I think so," she said.

Jack looked through the grate as well. The other side looked like a treasure trove, with chests of jewels, ancient artefacts, priceless paintings and sculptures. The next room he glanced into was full of weaponry, and there, to one side, were their weapons — the mirrored shield, Danny's bow and Jack's sunsteel sword. He gripped the

vent with his fists, and pulled it loose. Serenade dropped into the room and tossed up their weapons. She grabbed herself a couple of daggers and a new katana. Jack surveyed the other pieces of equipment with unease.

The Sisterhood are well armed enough to cause a lot of damage. They have to be stopped!

As they continued on their way through the narrow tunnels, Jack's hopes began to rise. It looked like they might get off the island alive. Then it was just a case of contacting Team Hero HQ and warning them what they'd discovered. With enough reinforcements, they could overpower the Sisterhood and take them into custody and—

"Wait!" said Danny, stopping ahead. "I hear something." He pointed along a branching tunnel. "Mercia."

"We don't have time," said Serenade. "We're not far from the vehicle bay."

Jack shared a glance with his friends. "If there's a chance to take down Mercia, we have to," he said. Ruby nodded, and they followed Danny. After a pause, Serenade followed.

"She won't let us live if she catches us again."

"That's just a risk we have to take now," said Jack.

Soon he could hear Mercia's voice himself, with no need for Danny's enhanced ears.

"... actually a blessing them coming here," the leader was saying. "We can lure Chancellor Rex to us. With him out of the way, Hero Academy itself will be an easy target. Think of all the technology and artefacts in its vault."

Jack's blood was boiling as they reached a vent and looked through.

In the room below, several members of the Sisterhood stood facing Mercia. All were dressed in combat suits of whites and greys and pale blues, perfect for blending in with the icy Arctic landscape of the island. One asked, "Do you think the Chancellor will come here?"

"He'd do anything for his precious students," Mercia said, rubbing her hands together. "And when I have him in captivity, I'll use him for his ability. Imagine being able to see into the future! We can make plans knowing we can never be caught. There will be no limits to what we can achieve!"

"What about the kids in the cold cells?" asked the other woman.

"What about them?" asked Mercia.

"We don't need them any more. They can freeze to death for all I care."

With that, she turned and strode away, trailed by her Sisters.

"Change of plans," whispered Ruby. "We have to stop Chancellor Rex coming here. Is there a communications console where we can get a message to him and warn him this is a trap?"

"That's your problem," said Serenade. "I got you out of the cells — you're on your own now."

Her face was hard, but Jack had already seen there was a softer side to Serenade.

"You can't mean that," he said. "If Mercia gets away with this, she'll just do something worse next time. And if she has Rex, who knows where she'll stop. You can see she's out of control."

Serenade lowered her gaze. "She's too powerful. She has the whole Sisterhood in her grasp."

"She didn't have you," said Ruby. "And I sense the others aren't fully behind her either. You could help them realise how evil she is. The Sisterhood could be a force for good, like it was in the days of the first Noxx invasion."

Serenade shook her head, then

muttered, "I can't believe I'm doing this."

"So you're with us?" said Danny.

"For now," said Serenade. "The communication centre is normally only guarded by two Sisters. It should be easy enough to ... convince them to help us get a message out."

They set off again through the duct channels. Jack knew it was a race against time. Chancellor Rex would already be on his way, maybe in *Arrow*, the Team Hero jet. *And he has no idea what he's flying into ...*

After a few minutes of clambering, Serenade put a finger to her lips.

Ahead was a metal hatch.

"It's just through there," she whispered. "Get ready."

Jack went to the hatch. "On three," he mouthed. He held up one finger, then two, then he punched through the hatch and leapt into the room.

He saw at once they'd made a mistake, but before he could tell the others, they flooded in behind him.

At least a dozen of Mercia's warrior Sisters waited on the other side of the room, standing in front of an array of complex-looking communications equipment. They wore armoured bodysuits, and carried an array of

weapons, ranging from Sai daggers
and nunchucks to katana blades.

And they all looked ready to use
them.

CHAPTER 3

THE SISTERS ATTACK

JACK ARCHED his back as a samurai
sword whistled past his nose. He raised
Blaze two-handed and threw himself
into action. Ruby raised her arms and
caught a blow from a fighting pole
on the face of her mirrored shield.
She charged, roaring, into a crowd
of the enemy, scattering them back.

Danny swung his bow, desperately trying to keep the attackers from swamping him, while Serenade moved like a stealthy shadow, kicking and punching her former accomplices. But there were just too many, and one of them managed to grab her and haul her to the ground.

Jack deflected a sword-slash with his own blade, sending it flying into a piece of equipment. Fizzing sparks showered his head. "We don't want to fight you!" he cried, but above the sound of clashing weapons, grunts and cries, he was pretty sure his voice was lost. An arm wrapped round his neck from behind, and legs looped round his waist as his attacker jumped on to his back. A Sister came at him as he flailed, thrusting with her forked daggers. Jack stumbled back, hit a wall and heard the woman clinging to him moan. He managed to prise her arm from his throat. With a heave, he tossed her across the room, where she smashed into a console and rolled off.

"Please!" he said, holding out his golden hands. "Stop this!"

The answer he got was a crossbow bolt hitting the wall right beside his head. The Sister who'd fired it was trying to reload, but the mechanism was jammed. She dropped the weapon and ran at him, leaping into a flying kick. It caught him in the gut and he fell to the ground, unable to suck in a breath. The woman raised her foot to stamp his head, but Danny rugby-tackled her aside.

Jack stood up as a fire-beam streaked from Ruby's eyes and heated a katana blade to red hot, forcing the bearer to let go with a wail. Serenade had struggled free from her captors. Using her super speed, she ran up and along a wall, almost defying gravity, and landed behind three of the Sisters. Dropping and thrusting out a leg, she felled them all.

Danny fired an arrow and it hit a Sister in the chest. She spasmed and collapsed.

He's set them to stun only, Jack realised.

The remaining warrior women weren't ready to give up. Nunchucks spun in a dizzying blur towards Jack. Pressed in a corner, with nowhere to go, he reached out a hand and grabbed them in mid-air. With a squeeze, he crumbled them to dust in front of his enemy's astonished face.

One of Mercia's soldiers had picked up Blaze though, and brandished the sunsteel sword with skill, hefting the blade aloft. She was about to hack Danny in half when a fire-beam shot a fraction past her ear, carving a scorch mark up the wall behind. The woman stumbled back in shock.

"I missed on purpose," said Ruby fiercely. "Don't test me."

The Sister lowered Blaze, then let it drop to the floor.

Across the room, Mercia's women were picking themselves up. None looked seriously hurt beside grazes and bruises, but suddenly they seemed less keen to fight on.

Danny nocked an energy arrow. "I've

turned up the voltage," he warned.

Serenade's blurred shape shot between the startled Sisters, picking up their discarded weapons before coming to a sudden halt at Jack's side. He allowed his breathing to steady as the golden power faded from his hands.

"What do you want?" said the Sister who'd wielded Blaze.

"To send a message," said Ruby. But as she approached the smoking, smashed-up communications consoles, Jack already had a sinking feeling that was already a lost cause.

"The comms are completely

wrecked," Ruby said.

"That doesn't surprise me," said Danny. "We just had World War Three in here."

"So much for the plan," said Jack. "Now we can't warn the Chancellor."

"I don't know why you're worried about him," said the lead Sister. "Mercia will never let you leave here alive."

"She wouldn't be the first to try to kill us," snapped Ruby. "People are always underestimating Team Hero."

While Danny kept his bow trained on the captives, Jack took a closer look at the comms. "Is there any way we can fix this?"

"Not in time," said Ruby. She turned to the lead Sister, eyes blazing. "Where has Mercia lured Chancellor Rex?"

The woman laughed. "You think I'd tell you? Your eyes may shoot fire, but we know the Team Hero code. You'd never harm an unarmed prisoner."

Serenade drew her daggers and pointed them at the woman's throat. "The girl might have a conscience, Allia, but what about me? I think I could get you to talk."

"We won't torture people," said Jack sternly.

"Speak for yourself," said Serenade,

pressing a blade against the skin of their captive.

Allia simply laughed. "Poor Serenade!" she said. "I'm far more scared of Mercia than your threats. You've seen what she can do. If any of us talk, she'll put us in a cold cell with our worst fear for the rest of our miserable lives. Kill me if you must — I'd rather that than feel our mistress's wrath."

The others nodded in agreement, and Jack's hopes hit rock bottom. *They're completely in thrall to Mercia. Terrified of her power. Prisoners in their own minds.*

Which meant there was only one way to convince them to help.

"Listen," he said. "You admit that Mercia is cruel. But what if she wasn't the leader any more?"

"Nice try," said Allia, "but it's impossible. No one crosses Mercia."

"I did," said Serenade quietly. "And now I'm putting my faith in Team Hero. Mercia makes us weaker, controlling us through fear, but together we can be strong, like Jack and his friends."

Allia didn't reply, but from the glances shared between the other sisters, Jack thought the message might actually be getting through.

"Join us," he said. "Tell us where Mercia is heading to intercept Chancellor Rex. We can stop her, and then you'll be free."

Allia took a deep breath. "The Shattered Coast," she said quietly. "That's the rendezvous point."

"But you'll have to be quick," said another. "Your Chancellor will be there soon."

"Thank you!" said Jack. "You won't regret helping us."

"It's not us I'm worried about," said Allia. "If I know Mercia, you're all going to die."

CHAPTER 4

FACING FEAR

AFTER ONE of the Sisters had retrieved their thermal gear, they rushed to the vehicle bay.

"How will we get there?" asked Jack, as they arrived in the hangar. "Is there a chopper?"

"Mercia will have taken it," said Serenade. "But we have something else."

She rushed to where a large object was covered with a sheet. Gripping the edges, she tore it off.

It looked like a cross between a speedboat and a giant skidoo, six or seven metres long, with huge gleaming metal runners on each side. Serenade sprang up on to the deck, climbed into the front seat and began to flick the switches on the control panel. Jack and his friends climbed aboard too.

Ahead of them, a section of what looked like rocky wall split, and two concealed doors slid apart.

"Strap in," said Serenade. "It's going to be a bumpy ride."

Jack took the fur-lined seat beside Serenade, and Ruby and Danny occupied the ones behind. They all buckled their harnesses, then the craft's engines roared and they lurched forward at astonishing speed.

They slid down, then sped across the icy white plain beyond. A 3D holographic map displayed on the console, with the skidoo appearing as a flashing red dot. Serenade pointed to a jagged section of topography. "That's where we're headed." She yanked the controls and they turned almost ninety degrees, throwing up a wave of snow and ice chips.

Jack's teeth rattled as they bounced and floated across the landscape. Icy gusts blasted his face and he tried to focus on the map. The thought of Chancellor Rex walking into a trap with a fiend like Mercia was almost too much to bear.

Why didn't Rex use his powers? He could have seen Mercia's plan!

Serenade killed the engine of their skidoo and they slid to a halt. "We go on foot from here," she said.

They all jumped off. Even through his thermal gear, Jack felt the cold at once, like a hand grasping him.

Together, they trudged up the

slope of a powdery dune. When they reached the top, the scale of the coast opened up before them in an epic vista. The water gleamed as it threaded its way into the coast like roots, and icebergs drifted offshore, some like mountains jutting from the waves, others shallower landmasses lined with cracks. Right on the edge of the shore Mercia waited alone in a field of ice boulders.

There was no sign of *Arrow* or Chancellor Rex.

We made it in time!

"It's four against one," said Ruby. "Let's do this."

"I don't like it," said Danny. "Why did she come alone?"

"I suppose she didn't want to spook the Chancellor," said Jack.

"And she probably knows her power is enough to stop him," said Serenade.

They ran side by side down the other side of the dune, and Mercia saw them coming when they were still fifty metres away.

"Well, well," she said. "You escaped the cold cells. Maybe I shouldn't have doubted you, Serenade."

"It's over," said Jack. "Throw down your weapons and come with us."

Mercia's shrill laughter was as

chilling as the Arctic air.

"I assure you," she replied. "It has only just begun. Sisters! Arise!"

Three of the boulders around her unfolded to reveal warrior women in white combat suits. Each carried what looked like a flame-thrower — a low-slung weapon with a long barrel.

Serenade gasped. "It's her elite guard," she said.

Mercia herself raised her arms. Long blades slid out along her sleeves, with spiked gauntlets sliding over her hands. "It looks like your Chancellor will see your dead bodies sooner than expected," she snarled. "Attack!"

Jack drew Blaze and ran straight at Mercia. But before he could reach her, one of her guards fired her weapon. It wasn't fire that erupted from the barrel though, but a beam of blue light that exploded the ground in front of him into a white mist. He pushed through it, but ran face-first into a solid wall, bouncing off and landing on his backside. The fogginess cleared to reveal a barrier of ice, freshly formed.

Ice-throwers!

Despite his shock, he wondered what Professor Rufus at the Academy would make of such tech.

Time to think about that later ...

Jack jumped up, and headed around the edge of the wall, only to be met with another blast, forming a second wall that joined the first. And before he knew what to do, he was completely surrounded by a prison of icy walls.

Growling, he sheathed Blaze and let his hand power up.

You don't stop Team Hero that easily!

He drove his fist through the wall, shattering it into fragments, then trod over the remains.

Serenade was leaping from spot

to spot to avoid the frigid blasts of
her attacker, but Danny was already
pinned to the ground, his legs encased
in ice. Ruby rushed to his side,
focused her eye-beams and melted the
ice to slush. Danny scrambled free.

"Thanks— Hey! Look out!"

Ruby turned as one of the elite guard fired a stream of ice at her, then lifted her shield. The stream bounced off, smashing right back at their attacker. Jack saw her freeze, turn blue, then fall over stiffly, still clutching the ice-blaster.

One down.

The other two Sisters advanced with Mercia.

"I'll handle this," said Danny. He loaded an arrow and fired into the air in a steep arc.

"You missed!" said Serenade.

"Wait ..." said Danny.

Jack watched as the arrow dipped in its trajectory. The Sisters had to jump aside as it slammed into the ice where they'd been standing, and the snow exploded. More cracks spread through the ice floe, and Jack felt the ground shift beneath his feet. The Sisters jumped from portion to portion, closing in, but Ruby jetted fire at their feet, melting the ice further.

"Careful!" said Serenade. "This whole shelf is unstable."

As if to prove her point, a whole section between them and their enemies suddenly crumbled away, leaving a channel several metres wide and cutting them off. Danny loaded another arrow, but before he could fire, a piercing screech cut through the air. Jack could barely follow the diving blue shape, but as it slammed into Danny's back he realised it was Mercia's Arctic falcon. Danny sprawled on the ice, dropping his weapons, as the bird tore at his tunic with its hooked beak.

"Help me!" he cried, managing to stand, flailing madly.

Jack picked up the fallen ice-thrower, took aim and fired. The blast ripped the falcon from Danny's back, and it dropped to the ice with a heavy thud.

"You'll regret that," shouted Mercia.

"Come and fight me," Jack retorted, running to stand at the edge of the channel that separated them. "I'm not scared of you!"

"You may not fear me, but you certainly fear something," said Mercia. "Let's see what."

Jack saw blackness well across the whites of her eyes, then the beams streaked forth. He ducked, but he realised they weren't aimed at him after all. To one side, they struck the ice, and from the wreaths of rising black smoke, a figure formed. Jack took a step back. *It can't be!*

The black smoke cleared to reveal a boy who looked exactly like him, a mirror image. But this Jack wore a black bodysuit, and the sword he carried had a black blade, like it had been dipped in tar. His eye were completely white, with blood-red pinpricks for pupils.

"I don't understand ..." Jack muttered.

"Yes, you do," said the boy. He sneered, and in the curl of his lips Jack saw traces of his old enemy General Gore, leader of the dark forces of Noxx. "I am what you will become," continued the reflection. "Just as Wulfstan Hightower turned to the ways of shadow, so will you. Good always turns to evil, as day becomes night."

"Never!" said Jack. The story of Wulfstan had haunted him since he'd first learned it — the original hero, who'd lost his way. *That won't happen to me!*

His tortured thoughts were interrupted, as his alter ego lifted his black blade and charged.

CHAPTER 5

SHADOW SELF

YOU'RE NOT real, thought Jack. *You're just an illusion ...*

Evil Jack grimaced, revealing rotten teeth. "Embrace your hatred," he hissed. "It will make you more powerful."

"I don't hate you," said Jack. "You're not even real!"

Evil Jack delivered a vicious kick to Jack's stomach. He flew backwards and crashed down on to the ice. He saw Danny and Ruby battling the other Sisters, while Serenade and Mercia squared off too, their glinting blades whirling and clashing.

Jack got to his feet as his evil twin came at him. Jack waited for his moment, then drove Blaze's point into the ice at his feet, sending a snaking crack under Evil Jack's feet. His enemy's mouth opened in shock, then he tumbled in, sinking under the water quickly. Jack walked to the edge and stared down into the blackness. A few bubbles broke the surface, then ceased.

"Good riddance," Jack said.

A movement in the sky made him look up. A dark shape streaked above them through the clouds.

Arrow! Chancellor Rex is here ...

Jack saw Serenade sliding across the ground, her katana skittering into the water. Mercia, alone, stared up at *Arrow* with a hateful glint in her eye.

Jack made to step towards her, but he saw movement under the surface of the water. Something caught his ankle and he fell in. Hands sought his neck, and he came face to face with

Evil Jack. He grabbed the other boy's throat as well. They both squeezed, turning in the water. Jack focused all his power into his fingers, clinging to consciousness. But the force on his own neck only increased as well.

We're evenly matched. We'll kill each other if we carry on like this …

Through the water above, he saw the blurred shapes of his friends above. *They're waiting for me.*

And that was when he realised. He and his evil twin weren't evenly matched at all. Because he had Ruby, and Danny, and all of Team Hero behind him. And the boy he was fighting had no one at all.

Remembering that made his super strength even stronger. Just as his lungs were ready to give in, he felt the fingers on his throat weaken. Evil Jack broke apart into black tendrils, carried away by the water. With the last of his energy, Jack kicked towards the surface, but he didn't have the strength to break through. For a moment he floated, resigned to death, then hands grabbed his armpits and hauled him out.

He floundered, shivering, on the ice, and saw Chancellor Rex standing over him.

"Jack!" he said. "Are you all right?"

"I think so," said Jack. His clothes were heavy with water, and he could barely move his numb fingers.

"She's getting away!" said Ruby, rushing towards them with Danny and pointing.

Jack saw Mercia was already charging up the snow dune back towards her helicopter. Serenade limped after her, carrying an ice-blaster. "Come on!" said Jack, grabbing Blaze from where he'd driven it into the ice.

He joined the chase, but as they reached the summit of the dune,

Mercia was already climbing on board her chopper. Danny fired an arrow, but missed. "My fire's run out," said Ruby, her dull orange eyes filled with despair.

Serenade pointed the ice-blaster at the chopper as its rotors began to spin, sending chips of ice flying out in all directions like shrapnel. The helicopter rose into the sky.

"It's not enough!" said Serenade. "She'll escape!"

Suddenly, from the other side of the helicopter, more blue streams erupted, and Jack saw several Sisters, armed with blasters, lending their freezing barrage to the assault.

They've decided not to live under Mercia's spell of fear any longer!

Ice coated the landing pads and the fuselage, making the craft shudder under its weight. In the cockpit, Mercia was fighting with the controls. She rose suddenly, but the ice streams followed the movement, and the helicopter tipped to one side. Like a bee drunk with nectar, the craft swayed off course over their heads before the rotors jammed with a grinding sound. The helicopter dropped lazily, and Jack looked away as it hit the water with a tremendous splash. When he glanced back, he saw bubbles frothing around the craft. Jack took a few steps towards the crash site, but Chancellor Rex held him back.

"There's nothing you can do for her now," he mumbled.

The sea swallowed the remains of the fuselage and Mercia did not emerge.

One by one the Sisterhood joined them, staring dumbly over the ice floe.

"She's gone," said Serenade quietly.

"What on Earth happened here?" asked Chancellor Rex.

"I'll make you a deal," said Danny,

hugging himself. "Find me a hot water bottle and I'll tell you everything."

Rex piloted *Arrow* back towards the Sisterhood's base to organise the loading up of stolen artefacts. None of the female warriors seemed in a mood to argue. Jack and his Team Hero friends found fresh clothes in the hold, and explained to their headmaster how the *Lancer*'s grounding had unfolded, and their subsequent encounters with the Sisterhood and Mercia. Ruby urged him to be forgiving towards the defeated Sisters.

"Mercia forced them to be thieves and mercenaries using her nightmarish visions. They were in her power. But when it came to it, they sided with us."

"You did well," said Chancellor Rex. "We located the *Lancer*'s signal. She's adrift, but all crew are accounted for. Captain Harrah is in a rather bad mood though."

Ruby laughed. "I've never seen him in a good mood."

The headmaster wagged his finger, failing to hold back a smirk. "Careful! If he hears that he'll have you court-martialled for insubordination!"

Jack saw Serenade sitting apart from everyone else, looking glum, and excused himself. She glanced up as he walked over. In her hands was the exquisite jewelled crown she'd stolen from the Ventura City Museum.

"I spent too long as a thief," she said. "It's only stuff, really, isn't it?" She handed it to him. "Take it back where it belongs."

"What will you do now?" he asked her.

"The Sisterhood will have to disband," she said, shaking her head. "We'd need a good leader to fix what Mercia has turned us into. But I don't think any of us are up to the task."

Jack smiled. "I don't know, I can think of someone who could give it a good try."

She looked over at him and frowned. "Me? That's crazy."

"No, it isn't," said Allia, walking over. "I can't think of anyone better."

"Mercia ruled through fear," said Chancellor Rex. "But with the right guidance, the Sisterhood can once again be a force for good."

"He's right, Serenade," said Allia. The other Sisters gathered in around them. "If there's one thing Team Hero have taught us, it's that when people work together and for each other, they can do amazing things."

Serenade slowly nodded. "Together, then," she said. "For each other." When she looked over at Jack, her smile matched his own and everyone else's.

Jack's chest swelled with pride, and he blushed as he glanced at his best friends. Team Hero would face more threats, he was sure, but if they did so side by side, there wasn't an enemy anywhere who could defeat them.